DISNEY
CLASSIC
POOH

Pooh's Cleanup

by Lauren Cecil
illustrated by Andrew Grey

Grosset & Dunlap
An Imprint of Penguin Group (USA) Inc.

Library of Congress Control Number: 2010010154

ISBN 978-0-448-45558-7   10 9 8 7 6 5 4 3 2 1

It was Piglet's birthday, and Winnie-the-Pooh had decided to do something very special for his little friend. He threw Piglet a marvelous birthday party and invited Christopher Robin, Tigger, Eeyore, Rabbit, Owl, Kanga, and Roo.

"Happy birthday, Piglet!" everyone hollered when
Pooh brought out a homemade honey cake.

After the party was over and everyone had left, Pooh looked around his house. It was in tatters.

"Oh bother," Pooh sighed. "How am I ever going to clean all this up?"

Pooh's rug was dirty, so he took out a broom and dustpan.

But try as he might, Pooh just couldn't get the rug clean.

Pooh's floor was sticky. So he got out his mop and then filled a bucket with soapy water.

Pooh tried to wash the floor, but the soap made it too slippery!

"Perhaps I can pick up all the dirty dishes," Pooh said. "But it'd be a shame to throw away all this cake."

So Pooh ate the leftover cake, which left one plate very clean indeed.

But there was still so much work to do . . .

Pooh tried to neaten up the couch, but all that cake and cleaning had made him quite tired.

"I'll just rest here for a moment," said Pooh. "Then I'll get back to cleaning."

Just as Pooh had drifted off to sleep, his friends knocked on the door.

"Did you forget something?" Pooh asked.

"Yes!" replied Christopher Robin. "We forgot to help you clean."

"Splendid!" said Pooh.

MR SANDERS

RNIG
ALSO

"How can I help?" Owl asked.

"You could clean the rug," Pooh said.

"Certainly!" said Owl as he flew the rug outside to give it a shake.

"What can we do?" Piglet and Roo asked.
"You can help me wash the floors," Pooh replied.
This was an especially good job for Piglet and
Roo. They could scrub the hard-to-reach places.

"What about me?" Tigger asked.

"Perhaps you could help me straighten up the couch," Pooh replied.

"Yippee!" Tigger cried. He bounced on Pooh's pillows, making them fluffier than ever!

With all his friends' help, Pooh's house was spick-and-span in no time at all!

"Thank you!" Pooh said. "My home has never been cleaner!"

"I say," Owl began, "your house looks so nice, it'd be perfect for another party!"

"And I don't even need to send out invitations," Pooh said. "Because all my friends are already here!"